UNLIMITED GRACE

UNLIMITED GRACE

Back In His Arms

MELISSA HAMLETT

Superior Publishing LLC.

Contents

Jordyn L. Crayton   1

1   The Meeting   3

2   Connections   10

3   The Union   19

4   The Commitment   26

5   The Reality   33

6   Beast Mode   41

7   Self-Destruction   47

8   Revelation   56

9   Redemption   63

About The Author   66

SUPERIOR PUBLISHING LLC. 2022
Cedar Bluff, MS 39741
(662) 295-9893

Jordyn L. Crayton

Jordyn Layla Crayton, the name given to me at birth. I am the baby of four children. My parents, Daniel and Rebecca Crayton, reared all four of us in a Christian home. We were taught about the Trinity. What is the Trinity? God the Father, Jesus Christ the Son, and the Holy Spirit that gives us power, knowledge and wisdom.

We were avid church goers. We attended Sunday School, Bible Class, B.T.U and Worship service on Sundays. I wasn't just a pew member. I was active in different departments of the church. I sang in the choir, worked on the youth Usher Board and was even a part of the praise team all that I took great joy in being a part of. I took part in every program a church could have every year, Christmas, Easter, Children Day whatever the church had. I wasn't jumping up and down to participate, but being a child of Daniel and Rebecca, you had no choice. They, my parents, believed whole-heartedly, "Train up a child in the way he should go, and when he is old, he will not depart from it. Proverbs 22:6" So they trained us and instilled in us moral and ethical values, that would get us through life.

My father would always say, "I'm not going to be with you always. You need to know how to maneuver your way through life." Daddy was a military man. He spent thirty years of his life serving in the Marines. He was a strong disciplinary that taught his children discipline, hard work, respect and most importantly love.

Growing up in a Christian home wasn't always easy. There were things we were exposed to outside the home that looked appealing to us. Like most children, there were things that we wanted to be involved in that our parents didn't approve of. The desire to be a part of these activities became more prevalent in my teenage years, the house parties, slumber parties with friends and even sometimes we weren't allowed to even visit some of our friends. Were my parents too hard on us? At times I thought they were. I never questioned my parents' decisions even when I didn't agree with them. I was taught that God has a purpose for everything He does. My father was the priest of our home. I'm not applying or alluding to the idea that my father was God. I'm just saying that he was the head of our house. There was a beneficial purpose behind everything he did.

The great question in this introduction is this, how did a woman that was raised to love God and others become so bitter and angry even to the point that she walked away from all that she believed and was taught? As you continue to read, you will be awakened to how clever and crafty Satan can be if you allow him to be.

Chapter 1

The Meeting

2005, I graduated Cum laude from the University of Pennsylvania. My major was marketing. It was something that I had always been interested in throughout high school. And since I lived in Philadelphia, the University of Pennsylvania was a good fit for me. I could have easily commuted but I preferred to stay on campus in order to get that campus life experience. My parents both agreed that it would be good for me to live on my own to get a taste of how life would be.

After graduation, I took three months off just to relax my mind. I had spent the last five years of my life dedicating myself to school and my studies. I didn't take a summer off; I just went year-round. I was determined not only to make my parents proud but I wanted to be proud of myself. I'm here to tell you, it wasn't easy at all but I can say it was worth it. It was always something going on that could easily get your mind distracted and cause you to not focus. Often, I think back to the pep talk my father gave me the day I moved in on campus.

"Now Jordyn we didn't send you here to party, goof off or become a mother before time. You are here to get an education. I want you to stay prayed up, stay focused and keep your eyes on the prize.

You have time after you have completed your assignment to do some of those things that I know you're itching to discover right now. You're going to meet and come in contact with people that won't be as dedicated or as committed as I know you're going to be. Stay away from those type of people and link up with people that are trying to succeed like you. Success demands work. It won't be handed to you but the opportunity is here. Take advantage of it and it will never disappoint you. "

Every time I got ready to step out of the boundaries that I had set for myself, those words would play in my head. I can't tell you how many times I wanted to throw a book to the side and just throw caution in the wind. How many times I had to pray to get through the temptation of wanting to attend a frat party. I don't want to falsely mislead you into thinking that all I did was keep my head in a book. There were times when some friends and I would go catch a movie and do a dinner afterwards. The University had plenty of activities that I did attend that boosted my moral. I didn't want to get myself caught up in anything that wasn't serving a greater purpose for me and what I was trying to accomplish.

My three months were up and I had begun to submit applications. I was ready to leave Philadelphia and start somewhere fresh and new! I got replies from many Marketing companies in many different states. The starting pay for low entry level employees sucked in my opinion. I knew I wasn't going in making tons of money, but I felt my resume was impressive. Plus, I had done some intern work at a local marketing firm as part of my credits for school.

Every day I would check my email to see if anything new had come in pertaining to my job search. I had begun to get frustrated. I had a Master's degree and graduated Cum laude with some experience. I didn't think it would be that hard to land a job that would pay me a decent salary. What did I do? I prayed about it. I asked God to open a door that would pay me enough money to live on my own. It was exactly three weeks later, I checked my email and there it was, A company out of New York, Brooks and Bracs Marketing Firm. They were in need of a Social Media Marketing Manager. It wasn't really what I wanted but it was a start. I called the firm to make sure I was seeing correctly. Eighty thousand was the starting pay. After talking with some lady named Linda Vize, I got off the phone shouting, "Yes, yes!"

"What in the world?" my mother was asking as she stood at my bedroom door.

"They want me to come to New York for a face-to-face interview." I said dancing all around the room.

"Who wants you to come?" My mother asked with her hands on her hips. Excitedly I responded,

"The marketing firm from New York Brooks and Bracs!"

"Where in New York?" my mom was asking with a confused look on her face.

"New York New York, Ma this is my chance! They are going to start me off with $80,000 a year and a raise after 3 months if all works out of course! It's better than the thirty and forty thousand the other companies were offering. They really weren't offering much. One agency had the nerve to tell me they had an opening in the mail room, can you believe that?" My mother stood in the door with a slight frown on her face. She let out a big sigh,

"Well Jordyn you have to start somewhere, maybe from the mail room you could have eventually moved up to where you want to be."

"Mom I am a college graduate! I am intelligent with a lot of bright ideas! These are not the slave days! And I didn't work as hard as I worked in school to end up in nobody's mail room. Sorry not sorry!"

"So, you're going to New York?"

"Yes, with your blessings as well as Dad's."

Later that night we all sat around the dinner table discussing my trip to New York. I could tell my father was not really thrilled about it but he never opposed it either. I explained that the lady Linda ask me when did I think I could be there. I asked her when did they want me to be there? It was only a 2-hour drive and I could go and come back the same day or the next day. This is when my father stepped in to throw his weight around.

"I'm not letting you to go to New York by yourself. It's too much going on and I would feel better knowing you were accompanied by your mother and I."

I knew my father well enough to know that he was determined to go. His tone was final and there was no need for me to explain my position or how I felt. As I laid in my bed, later on that night wrapped in my thoughts, I thought about how good God had been to me. I thought about all the sacrifices I had made to get me to where I was in life. I wasn't the perfect child. I never gave my mother and father the headaches, or drama other children gave their parents. I was almost twenty-four years old and my parents still treated me like a kid. I thought I had more than proven myself as being responsible. Instead of them being happy about the potential job opportunity, they were more concerned about me being in New York. I understood New York was a big city and that awful things were happening in the world. But I felt that something could have just as easily happened to me in Philadelphia. Twenty-three years old and I was being escorted by my parents. Where do they do that at? I prayed and begged God to let me get the job. Deep down I was looking forward to being miles away from my parent so I could live my life. I deserved to be free and happy.

In New York

We arrived in New York, New York on a Monday morning. My interview was scheduled at 9:00 A.M. I went in with a prayer and confidence. I was interviewed by a balding short dumpy Caucasian male. At first sight, I said to myself,

"He looks mean. He looks like he doesn't like black people." I still didn't know whether or not he liked black people but he treated me with the utmost respect and was very kind. The interview lasted about 45 minutes. He excused himself from the room and told me he would be right back. While he was gone, I took the time to observe the office. It was huge with a nice oak desk that sat in the middle. I looked at all the plaques and pictures on the wall and some that were on his desk. There was a big window right behind the nice letter chair he sat in. The view was spectacular. I started getting nervous because it seemed as though he was taking forever to return. I heard the door open behind me and I looked back to see the man that interviewed me along with another Caucasian man.

"This is Mr. Robert Kapp. We call him Bob around here." I heard my interviewer saying. I jumped up quickly because Mr. Kapp was extending his hand for a handshake. As soon as our hands disconnected, I heard Mr. Kapp say welcome to Brooks and Bracs I wasn't sure if he was welcoming to the job or just welcoming me to the building. So, I blurted out the question,

"Do I have the job?"They both looked at each other and in unison they said,

"Yes!" My legs felt light under me. I hadn't realized that I was so tense. The smile that registered on my face was that of complete Joy. God had come through for me again. My mom would say God's grace is so amazing. I couldn't wait to get to the elevator. As soon as I got in, I called my dad,

"Hello!" his deep baritone voice answered.

"I got it! I got it! I got it! I got the job!"

"Congratulations baby girl! I'm proud of you where are you now?"

"I'm coming down the elevator. I'll be out there in about 5 minutes." Yes, my mother and father waited in the car while I had my interview. It would have been too embarrass-ing to tell but at that moment I didn't care. I had just got hired at a top notch marketing firm. Life for me was looking good and far as I was concerned it would only get better. I jumped in the car as soon as my dad drove it around.

"When they tell you to start?" My mom asked as I was adjusting my seat belt. I replied anxiously,

"I only have two weeks to find a place and get settled. They want me at work 2 weeks from today. Since it is only a little over 2 hours to drive, I can just commute until I find me a place to live."

I could see my dad looking at me in the rear view mirror. Everybody in the car got really quiet. The silence was broken when my mother said,

"We are going to try and find you somewhere to live today while we are here. Your father called up some old friends that recommended some reasonable apartments in nice neighborhoods."

"Wow!" I said, "When did all this take place?"

"When you were in there having your interview. Daniel was busy on the phone trying to get everything in place for you."

I felt somewhat guilty for wanting to get away from them. My parents were my backbone. They loved me unconditionally. I talked about making sacrifices but they made sacrifices as well. My dad wasn't able to make every piano recital every ballad performance or every school play. But he made sure he called before each one he couldn't make to give me that reassurance. His words were always,

"Baby girl you got this!"

Chapter 2

Connections

I had been at Brooks and Bracs for approximately six months. I liked my job but I didn't love my job. I had a little cubicle with a computer that sits on a desk. Along with ten other people that had the same cubicle, with the computer that sat on the desk. None of the people seem to be friendly. I had to constantly remind myself that I wasn't there to make friends. I wanted to pursue my career and make lots of money.

One day this white girl came to my cubicle and personally introduced herself. All of us wore name tags so I knew her name was Tiffany Royce. She was cute with a nice slim build. When she smiled you could see perfectly white even teeth. She mostly wore ponytails but I could tell her hair was shoulder-length.

"How do you like being the social manager?" She asked me. I shrugged my shoulders and told her,

" I guess it's okay." She gave me a half smile while shaking her head.

"Girl that's just a fancy name they give to the ones they want to hold accountable in case one of us messes up."

I didn't know if she was trying to get me into an argument or belittle me. Anyway I decided to take the high road and politely replied,

"I know my job requirements." She quickly apologize,

"I didn't mean to offend you. I've been working here for almost 5 years. I've seen these social managers come and go. Brooks and Bracs promised them one thing and they find out they don't deliver."

"Well they have given me what they promised. A job and the opportunity. So if you would be so kind and get back to your workstation, I would appreciate it."

I smiled as sweet as I could muster. With a toss of her ponytail she headed back to her cubicle. One of the requirements of my job was making sure all the other employees stay busy on their computers. She actually struck a nerve because I thought I would have my own office and not be on the floor working alongside everyone else. The day I started Mr. Kapp introduced me and told me that I was the new manager. Everybody was supposed to report to me with any concerns or problems. They also reported to me if they wanted to be off or if they weren't coming in. It was almost 5 P.M. It was time to shut the computers down and clock out. I had just finished logging out of my computer when Tiffany again appeared at my desk.

"Look I'm sorry. I feel like I rubbed you the wrong way. Let me make it up to you. Let's go get a drink. I know this great place that I go to all the time."

I put my hand up to stop her before she went on further.

"I don't drink plus it's a weekday. The only thing I want to do is go home take a hot shower and go to bed."

"You must have the most boring life."

"You don't know anything about me" I fired back. I didn't know who this white chick thought she was talking to but she had the right one.

"I'm trying to befriend you but it seems like I keep saying the wrong things. Maybe that's why I don't have a whole lot of friends."

I actually caught a glimpse of sadness in her eyes and I heard the choking in her voice. I started to rethink my response to her. She told me she had been there for almost seven years. It must have been hard to watch a company keep bringing people in over you. I wondered what type of credentials she had. Maybe she did just want to be friends. What if she was the person that God had put in my path to test me?

"I tell you what, If you're not busy Friday, maybe you and I can go to this place you were telling me about. I don't drink but we can get out and mingle with some other people. The only people I know here are the people I work with and my landlord."

"Really!" She squealed.

"Miss Crayton it is a date!"

"Jordyn" I told everybody to call me by my first name Jordyn.

Friday had come and Tiffany agreed to pick me up at my apartment. I'm not going to lie. I was actually excited. I had all those big plans of living life and having fun. Twenty-four years old and I was living like an old maid.

My job wasn't physical but it could sometimes be mentally draining. I wanted to be on the seventh floor. That was the floor where all the big executives worked. On that floor is where the minds worked to come up with campaign slogans for major corporations. They made the big money. The money I wanted to make some day. They also got commissions on top of those six-figure incomes. I made it my daily and nightly prayer for God to get me to that 7th floor. I can do all things through Jesus Christ who strengthens me, Philippians 4:13. My daddy taught me this verse at the age of four. I can recite it backwards if I had to.

The doorbell rang. I look at the time on my phone it was 8:00 P.M. Tiffany was right on time. I got up to the open the door and she was standing there in a skirt that was way too short. I took one look at her and asked her was she cold? She was very weird! The temperature outside was like 30 degrees. Tiffany was already about 5 ft 8 inches tall naturally. Those 4 inch heels made her tower over me like a giant. I was only 5'6 myself. I couldn't resist asking her are we going to a bar or a street corner?

"Whichever one you have a taste for tonight." she replied and we both laughed. I grab my purse and off we went. It only took 15 minutes to get to the bar from my apartment. I didn't know what to expect. It wasn't like I hadn't ever been in a bar before, because I had. I didn't know much about Tiffany but I sensed that she could be on the Wild Side. Thus, causing me to have a little apprehension of having high expectations of her hang out spots. But to my surprise, it was nice and clean looking. It was a grill and bar with a big dance floor in the middle. Booths, tables and chairs were lined up all around the room.

She and I took a seat at the bar. She ordered a gin and tonic. She ordered me soda cranberry and lime.

"It's good," she said, "since you don't drink." It didn't take the bartender long to whip the drinks up. Tiffany was right, the beverage had a nice taste and full of flavor. Tiffany and I were in the middle of a conversation when she jumped off the barstool and ran toward three men that had entered the bar. Two white guys and a fine and I do mean fine African-American brother. I had seen some good-looking guys in my lifetime but this guy could have made the front page of Jet Magazine. I could imagine the headlines saying, "Finest Black Man in the World." Tiffany was walking over to the bar with them. I was hoping my hair wasn't out of place or my lipstick wasn't smeared. She was introducing them,

"Jordan this is Brian Chris and Eric. Guys this is my boss Jordyn Crayton."

"Your boss!" One of them was saying,

"That's right! She is our manager for the social marketing department." The one named Brian was very cute. I could see how Tiffany was giggling and flirting with him that she really liked him. I was almost afraid to look at Eric. Surely a man this gorgeous already had somebody tucked away. Tiffany and Brian went to dance and I was alone with Eric and Chris. Then Chris quickly excused himself which left me alone with Eric.

"So Jordyn where are you from?" His voice was buttery and smooth. His caramel color skin looked flawless. It only added more appeal to his chiseled features.

"I'm from Pennsylvania, Philadelphia to be exact."

"Oh okay. How long have you been in New York?"

"Not long."

This man was asking me questions and I was finding it hard to talk. Get it together Jordyn I was saying in my head.

"Oh snap! That's the new song by Mario they're playing you want to dance?" I was sitting there staring like the man had asked me to do something out of the ordinary. He wanted me to dance not go to a deserted island with him. I said,

Sure!"

He led me to the dance floor. I hadn't heard the song before. It had an upbeat sound. Let Me Love You, by an artist named Mario. Eric twirled me around on that dance floor and I was matching his moves beat by beat. The smell of his cologne was mesmerizing. It was a light and fresh smell. The song ended and I was about to walk off the dance floor when he grabbed my hand and asked for another dance. They were playing the smooth sound of Kenny G. The beat of the song was a lot slower this time. I relaxed in Eric's arms as if that was where I was supposed to be. I was responding to him like a teenager with her first school crush. Maybe it was the smoke in the air, the atmosphere, or the way he held me. I don't know what it was. The only thing I knew for sure is that I didn't want the moment to end.

Tiffany had gotten wasted. She wasn't able to drive us home. Brian and Chris took Tiffany's car to drive her home which left me to ride in the car with Eric. I was taking notes as I watched him open the door for me. He had to be at least six feet tall and maybe two or three inches added to that. He had also been drinking but he didn't appear to be so intoxicated that he couldn't safely get me home. Once he was in the car buckled up and started the engine, I asked him was he okay to drive. He looked toward me and flashed me a smile and said,

"Oh, you're always safe with me baby. Just sit back and give me your address."

I gave him my address and we took off heading in that direction. Once we arrived at my apartment complex, I realized I wasn't ready to leave his presence. I wasn't ready to invite him in either. I had just met this guy and I wasn't comfortable inviting a stranger in my home. It was evident that he wasn't ready for the night to end either. He left the car running while we sat there and talked.

"So, Jordyn Crayton tell me more about you." He was saying to me as he was adjusting his seat to lay back.

"What do you want to know?" I asked.

"Are you dating anybody? Do you have any children? Are you on drugs? Are you a felon?"

We both started laughing at his line of questioning.

"No to all the above I'm twenty-four years old. A graduate from the University of Pennsylvania, Go Quakers! I have a master's degree in marketing and I graduated Cum laud."

Eric sat up and gave me a look that indicated that he was impressed. I don't know at this point if I had what people called the big head or not. I just know it felt good to share my credentials and accomplishments with others.

"I heard Tiffany say something about you are her boss."

"Yes, I'm the manager in the division of social media. That's not what I want to do long-term. I actually want to get to the place where I can create ads and showcase my talents. I didn't think it would be this hard starting out. But I have to start somewhere and I'm praying the opportunity will come for me to advance."

"What's the name of the company again

"Brooks and Bracs marketing firm. It's a very distinguished firm."

"I have a client that was in search of a good marketing company. His name is Philip Stewart. I work in corporate law."

I didn't give him time to finish before I blurted out, "You're a lawyer?"

"Dang is that a bad thing? Don't believe the hype all lawyers aren't crooked."   I gave him one of those exasperating looks before I responded. "Crooked never entered my mind."

I was impressed by the new found revelation. Not only was this brother fine but he was educated. It was a big plus in my book. I went from being intrigued to totally fascinated by this man.

"I don't think every lawyer is crooked just like I don't think all people are bad. To be honest I'm impressed. So, let me ask you a question, is there a special lady you have?"

"No special lady my dear. If there was one, I wouldn't be sitting here with you. "

I didn't see it coming. His lips were on my lips and my body began stiffening up due to the shock. It wasn't long before I found myself relaxing and giving in to the soft magnetic feel of his mouth locked with mine. When the kiss was over, he kissed my forehead and looked me straight in my eyes before he said,

"I have been wanting to kiss you all night. The moment I laid eyes on you, I wanted to know more about you."

I was at a loss for words. My heart was beating so fast. All kinds of thoughts were running through my head. He walked me to my door but not before we exchanged phone numbers. He leaned down to give me another kiss but this time it was on my cheek. He told me to be looking out for his phone call and he turned and walked away.

That night when I went to bed, all I could think about was Eric. The smell of his cologne still lingered in my mind. Over and over I kept thinking about everything that had transpired. I wanted to recapture every moment of the night. From the time he walked into the club, down to the moment he walked away from my apartment. I wasn't sure about love at first sight. I just knew it was something exciting I was feeling. That something had me thinking about Eric Jackson all night.

Chapter 3

The Union

I was sitting at my desk when Mr. Kapp's assistant entered the room and told me Mr. Kapp needed to see me in his office. I got up from my desk and followed her out the door down the hallway. Mr Kapp's office was the seventh on the 7th floor. The floor that I have been praying to get to one day. She and I reached the elevator. It was open and we stepped in, the assistant pushed number seven and we proceeded to go up from the third floor. I wasn't really too concerned about what Mr. Kapp wanted. I knew I was doing my job sufficiently.

My mind reverted back to Eric. He and I had been dating for the past six weeks. If other people profess to be on cloud nine, then I was on cloud 29. I was completely hooked on Eric Dontae Jackson. My Boo. My Man. My Heart. The elevator door open and we stepped out. We walk down the corridor to Mr. Kapp's office. The assistant knocked on his door but didn't enter until she heard his voice permitting us to come in. He stood up from his desk and gave his assistant permission to leave.

"Have a seat Miss Crayton." His tone was light and friendly sounding. I took a seat eager to hear what he wanted with me.

"Do you know a man by the name of Philip Stewart?" My mind began racing. I had heard that name before but I couldn't remember where I had heard it. So I decided to just be honest about it,

"I've heard the name but sorry I can't remember where I heard it from."

"Well he knows you or at least he knows of you. Let's put it that way." He came from around his desk to the front of his desk to stand before me. He had his arms folded with a look on his face that I couldn't quite describe.

"Mr. Stewart has chosen Brooks and Bracs to market his products."

"That's great!" I replied.

"He wants you to be on the team that's going to come up with the ad."

I wasn't sure I heard him right so I asked him,

"He wants me to work on the ad?"

"He said he wanted Jordyn Crayton to work on his ads. Now unless there is another Jordyn Crayton in the building somebody needs to let me know."

I wanted to get up and shout right then and there. I had been praying for this opportunity and now it had finally presented itself. All I could think about at that moment is that God is good and prayer works. I stood up an extended my hand for a handshake.

"Thank you Mr. Kapp! Thank you for this opportunity! I promise I will do my very best to make this company proud."

"You better, this is a multi million-dollar ad campaign selecting us was based on you being the lead person in charge. Evidently someone highly recommended you. You can finish out the rest of the day in the social media Department. But in the morning I want you to come on this floor and go to room C. Once you get there, Adrian Banks will fill you in on everything else."

I thanked Mr. Kapp once again. As I left the office, I felt so elated. My prayers were being answered. God favored me and it was a feeling like none other I had ever felt. The moment I made it to my desk, I unlocked my drawer, pulled out my purse and reached for my cellphone. The first person I called was Eric, I had to share my good news. My parents, siblings, and not even my good friend that lived in Virginia was my first call. It was Eric that was on my mind. I don't know if I was just looking for a reason to call him or not, I just really wanted to share my good news. I think it was a combination of both. I hadn't even said anything to Tiffany, I saw her look up from her computer with a questioning look on her face. I gave her the thumbs-up to let her know everything was okay. Eric's phone was ringing. He answered,

"Hello beautiful."

"Eric you will never guess what happened for me today!"

"Well why don't you just tell me what happened for my baby today."

"Eric they are moving me to the 7th Floor! I'm actually going to help develop and ad for some guy named Phillip Stewart. He told them he wanted me to be the lead person. I don't even know who Phillip Stewart is. But anyway, I start tomorrow. I think my daddy may have had a hand in it some kind of way."

"Hold on baby," Eric was like, "Don't you remember I told you I had a client that was looking for a great marketing company that could advertise their product? And that the reason he came to our law office was because there was a problem with the other marketing company he was using. I gave him the name of your firm and I told him to mention your name if he decided to go with Brooks and Brac's. I can't let you give that credit to anybody else."

It all started coming back to me. I remembered where I knew that name from. It was Eric that had mentioned the name. I had forgotten all about it. I remembered a lot about that night but that piece of information slipped my mind.

"That's right. You did tell me about this guy. I'm sorry boo. It just slipped my mind. I owe you a huge thanks. Thank you so much baby."

"No problem love. Let's celebrate tonight! We can go out catch a movie and do dinner."

"Sounds good to me babe. Let's say 7 or 7:30."

"You got a date Love. See you then, later."

Eric hung up. He told me that he never liked to say goodbye. He said goodbye sounded so final as if it was the end of contact. Eric had shared a lot with me over the weeks since we had been dating. He was only seven years old when his mother told him goodbye. That night she had been stabbed to death by another female she had an altercation with. His father dotted in and out of his life. After the death of his mother his aunt took his sister and him to raise as her own. His aunt was a school teacher and she believed wholehardheartedly in education. He chooses to look at his fate as a blessing. He gives his aunt and uncle the credit for being the man he is today.

As soon as I got home, I called my parents to let them in on my good news. They were happy for me and I knew they would be. My dad started questioning me about why I haven't been coming home like I used to. Every other weekend I would drive home to Philadelphia. This was due to the fact that I didn't know anybody in New York. I was lonely and yearned to be around family and friends. While I was on the phone I debated within myself whether to tell my father about Eric. I was too happy to let him spoil my joy by asking me 20,000 questions. I loved my father with every fiber of my being. At times, he could be too critical. I didn't know where my relationship with Eric was going so I opted not to tell him until I knew it was a sure thing.

Since Eric and I had been dating, I stopped going home every other weekend. He and I had plans every weekend. I wasn't lonely anymore. I had found someone to fill that void and pacify that yearning that had come over me. I had not been home in over a month. I simply told my father that I had been working to get to where I am now headed.

Our parents taught us not to lie. Lying had consequences and it will get you in some serious trouble. These are the words Daniel Crayton always told us. His words registered with us when my brother Isaiah got killed in an automobile accident. This tragedy shook the foundation of the Crayton household like it had never been shook before. Isaiah was my parents' second born child. He loved sports. He had been given specific orders to come home after basketball practice that Wednesday afternoon. He disobeyed my father and went riding with some of his friends. They found somebody in the neighborhood to buy them alcohol. The driver of the vehicle lost control going eighty miles per hour around the curve. He hit a bridge and all three were killed instantly.

I was ten years old and it was the scariest time of my life. I could hear my mother screaming all over the house. Isaiah was only sixteen years old. My oldest sister, Faith had just turned nineteen. My other brother Nyle was fourteen at the time. The only time I had ever seen my father cry is when he looked down on his son lying in the casket. I wasn't too quick to cry. I guess I got it from my father. My mom and Faith would cry at the drop of a dime. Nyle was just like me it took a lot to make tears come out of our eyes.

As soon as I hung up with my dad, I called Faith. Faith was my secret keeper. I could tell her anything. She was a lot like our mama. I was always a daddy's girl. She clung more to mama. She married while she was still in college. She got pregnant and had an old-fashioned shotgun wedding. Faith graduated and Tyrone and her are still together with four children. Now you understand why my daddy told me he wasn't sending me to school to become a mother before time. The older siblings always seem to make it harder for the younger ones.

"Jae what you got going on?"

My family and friends called me Jae the only time my dad referred to me as Jordyn is when he meant business. I started telling her about what happened at work. She was so happy for for me. I loved my big sister. We laughed about the time I used to call her mama. Faith took care of all of us while mamma worked and Daddy was deployed.

"How is everything with Mr. Eric?"

I had already told Faith all about Eric. She knew every-thing from A to Z. I was blushing over the phone but of course Faith didn't know. I answered back in a childlike voice,

"It's good girl! I think me in love!"

"Slow down a little sis, you don't know him well enough to be in love already." My voice change quick after she made that statement. I shot back,

"You were in college when you fell in love with Tyrone."

"I wasn't in love with Tyrone in college. I was in lust. There is a big difference. I grew to love Tyrone after we married because I got to know him and he got a chance to know me. I'm not trying to burst your bubble baby. I just want you to be sure about who you're dealing with and take it slow."

I knew Faith was right. Just like I knew she would never say or do anything to intentionally hurt me. She was look-ing out for me. That's what big sisters did. I loved her even more at that moment. I don't know what I would have done if I didn't have the love and support of my family.

Chapter 4

The Commitment

It was 2007 almost two years later and I had become a major player at the marketing firm. I finally got my own office and I was now making good money. I had upgraded to a six-figure income. They didn't just hand it to me, I worked hard for it. I put in long hours and worked some weekends if it was necessary. The company discovered what I already knew. I had talent, skills, determination and a commitment to the company. I had already pulled in five new companies for our firm to represent.

My advertising ideas were brilliant and eye-catching. Word about our company began to generate new clients from all over the world. The name Jordyn Crayton had began to ring in the ears of high-profile businessmen and women. I had to give credit to my fiance Eric for a lot of it. Yes I said fiance!

One night we were having dinner at this jazzy five star restaurant, I excused myself to go to the bathroom, when I came back there was a saxophone player playing the same song We danced to the first night we met. He wasn't Kenny G but he was a close second. Eric got up from the table, got down on one knee and asked me to marry him. Of course I said yes! Everyone in earshot of us started clapping and cheering us on. After dinner we enjoyed a beautiful carriage ride around the city.

Eric and I had already made several trips to my hometown. The first time my parents met Eric I was nervous. It wasn't my mother I was worried about. It was the that military dad of mine. As I had predicted. My dad began drilling Eric with questions after question. I had already prepared him for my Dad's military style of questioning. You would have thought Eric was putting in an application to work instead of dating his daughter. But Eric held his own. He was precise and very respectful. He showed my father he was a real man that could hold his own. No matter what subject my father brought up, Eric was able to speak intelligently on it. I was sitting at the dining room table watching and listening to these two men. Each one having a significant role in my life but in totally different ways.

Before Eric proposed to me, he had gone to Philadelphia by himself to ask my parents permission for my hand in marriage. I didn't even know until I called them to give them my good news and they said we already know. We knew before you did.

Planning a wedding wasn't as easy as I thought. I started getting very frustrated before Tiffany asked to let her help. Tiffany and I had became very close. I recommend her to take my position as Social Media Manager. Tiffany had some college experience but she didn't have a degree. I assured Mr. Kapp that Tiffany was more than capable of handling the job. Remember the saying, "When you move up reach down and pull someone else up?" I don't know if it was actually a saying but again it was something we were taught by our parents.

Faith and Tiffany finally got a chance to meet when Faith came to New York for the weekend. We sat in my living room discussing colors, flowers, cakes, catering, etc and everything else that goes with planning a wedding. Eric really didn't have too much input on things, but that was his choice. The one thing he did ask me was to have the wedding at his church in New York. I obliged his request but it did not sit well with my parents. They wanted me to come home and get married. Dad even took it upon himself to have a counseling session set up with the pastor for Eric and I. Eric wasn't having no part of it and to be honest neither was I. We loved each other and that's the only thing that truly mattered.

Faith and Tiffany assured me that they had everything under control. Faith and my mother we're coming up the following weekend so I could pick out my wedding dress. My friend Kasey was coming from Virginia. We were going to make it a girl's weekend. Tiffany suggested that we go ahead and have the bridal shower since everyone was already going to be in New York. Tiffany's heart was in the right place but I had aunts, nieces, and cousins that I wanted to be at my bridal shower. It would have been too short of a notice for them. After talking to Faith she suggested that since the wedding was going to be in New York, have the bridal shower in Philadelphia.

My sister rented a building only a couple of blocks from where I used to live. The minute I entered the room I was blown away. It was decorated so beautiful. Pink and silver for the colors. The tablecloths were pink and adorned with silver accessories. Each table had a silver centerpiece with pink candles and a crystal holder surrounding them. Mama and Faith had out-done themselves and I was again thanking God for giving me such a sweet family.

Some of my family I hadn't seen in a while, like some of my aunts and their daughters came from out of town just to share my special moment. Some promised me they would be back for the wedding. But others told me they probably wouldn't be able to make it back. I was still grateful they came to celebrate with me. We laughed, played games, ate and opened gifts.

Tiffany came and sat beside me.

"Our family is nothing like this." I looked at her,

"What do you mean like this?"

"We don't get together and do all this hugging and kissing. We barely speak to one another. It seems like the love you share is real." I felt somewhat sorry for Tiffany. I couldn't imagine not having a close knit family.

"I mean they just welcomed me in with open arms and they don't even know me."

"My family origin is from the South. Half the people you see in this room are either from Mississippi, Georgia or Tennessee. My father is originally from Mississippi. He ended up in Pennsylvania because of the military. Well that and my mother. My mother was born in Georgia. She left Georgia to come live with my aunt that stayed in Philadelphia. She later died but my mom decided to stay."

Tiffany let out a sigh before she looked at me and said,

"You are one blessed girl."

I smiled while looking around at everybody in the room and said,

"It's God's grace Tiff."

The Wedding Day

After months and months of planning, my wedding day had arrived. We booked a suite at the Commodore Hotel so it would be plenty of room for all of my female wedding party. We all were running around like chickens with our heads cut off. Tiffany was right by my side jumping up to get anything I needed. Faith had went to church to make sure everything was being handled properly. My mother and father stayed at my apartment. The hairdresser was putting on the finishing touches.

"Tiffany go call my parents and make sure they're okay." I yelled out

"I already called, Mr. Crayton said they were getting ready to walk out the door."

"What about Eric's aunt and uncle?"

"I called Eric and he said they were already at the church."

"What about my aunt,"

Tiffany cut me off before I could get another word out.

"Jae everything is in order stop worrying. We got you girl. This is your special day. Don't ruin it by worrying."

My body relaxed some. I noticed that Tiffany had referred to me as Jae. She had been around my family long enough to pick up on my nickname.

We had finally arrived at the church, my wedding planner was trying her best to get us all in position. She instructed me to go in a room where my father was. She made it clear that I was not to come out until she came and got me.

I opened the door and there my handsome father stood in his black tuxedo and silver bow tie. I closed the door behind me and went to give him a hug. I could feel the grip of his hug around my waist and back. It was almost as if he didn't want to turn me loose. He eased his grip and placed his hands around my shoulder and just looked at me as if he was looking at me for the first time.

"My baby girl, my heart and joy. I know you think I was super hard on you, the truth is, I was. I saw something in you Jordyn. I saw me in you. Out of all of my children you are more like me than any of them. You don't have that soft cushy interior like your sister and your mama. At least not until you met your husband-to-be. The first time you brought him to me meet us. I noticed a difference in you. Your mama said it was love and love softens you. I don't mind the softness but don't be so soft that you can't stand up for yourself if things don't work out. I'm not telling you anything that I didn't tell your sister on her wedding day. So I need you to listen to me. If for some reason you find yourself being mistreated, disrespected and not being taken care of, you leave. Do not stay anywhere you're not happy. If you find yourself afraid to leave, just call me. I'm only a phone call away. I need you to know that I'm going to always be here for you. I love you and I pray the best for you."

After his speech he kissed me on my forehead. Remember when I said, I didn't cry easily? At that moment tears trickled down my cheeks. My dad was the first man I had ever loved. I never saw him treat my mother with anything but respect.

As we walked down the aisle, my arm locked in my father's arm. I was only concentrating on one thing. It was the man that would soon be my husband. I had dreamed of this day so many times. I found myself standing at the altar beside my husband-to-be. I actually felt like I was in a fairy tale. I was Cinderella who had found my prince. Eric brought so much joy love and peace to my life. I felt like God was smiling down on us. Grace has brought us together and I just knew Grace would keep us together. I was committing myself to this man, for better, for worse, for richer or poorer in sickness and health. He and I were now under a covenant union before God.

Chapter 5

The Reality

It had been 10 years

since I stood before God, my family, and friends. I took my wedding vows seriously. Eric Dontae Jackson was the man I wanted to spend the rest of my life with. In 10 years a lot of things took place. I became a mother of three beautiful children. My son, Eric Junior, was nine. My daughters, Amari seven and Zoe five.

My father had passed away five years into our marriage. He had a massive heart attack in his sleep. I mourned a long time after his death. My husband kept telling me it was time to get over it. He just didn't understand the hurt I was feeling.

In the first couple of years of our marriage everything was going great. We bought a house in an upscale neighborhood. He and I used to do date night every weekend. But when the children started coming we went from every weekend to once a month to not at all. We started having little arguments that escalated into big arguments. We stopped communicating and went into silent mode. The children and bills were the only things we actually talked about. It was like we had lost our way to each other and didn't know how to get back.

I joined his church right after we got married. Eric never attended church every Sunday, even when we were dating. I kept stressing to him how important it was for us to go to church as a family. It was like talking to a brick wall. Eric wasn't listening to anything I had to say.

When I first saw the signs of our marriage being in trouble. I pleaded with Eric for us to go to counseling. He refused to even talk about it. I never told anyone about our marital problems. I didn't want anyone to know what we were going through. I constantly found myself praying to God. I loved my husband and my family and I was willing to do whatever it took to get us back where we used to be.

Eric's new position had him going out of town a lot. On the days he was out of town I was left to handle the children. Between taking care of the children and trying to maintain the household duties, I became overwhelmed. I ended up having to hire someone to come in to help with the children and the household. Eric didn't like it because he thought I should have talked to him about it first. One day we had gotten into another argument and he brought it up. We were getting ready to go to bed and I simply asked him if was he going to be able to pick Eric Junior up from his soccer practice.

"You hired a nanny, get her to pick him up!" He fired back.

"Eric what is really going on with you? I can't ask you a simple question without you getting bent out of shape. Why can't you pick him up?"

"I have a job Jordyn. I can't just walk out when I feel like it."

"I have a job too!"

"You wouldn't have had the job if it wasn't for me! Seems like you've forgotten who got you on the gravy train!"

There it was, I don't know how I could have been so blind not to see it. My salary along with my commissions put my income over the top. I was bringing in more money than Eric and evidently he was feeling some type of way about it. A couple of years before I was featured in a business magazine as one of the top 10 most influential women in the area. I was awarded with a plaque at their annual banquet. Eric was sitting down on the side of the bed. I walked over and sat beside him.

"Eric listen to me. It doesn't matter whether I make a million a week. You and I are one. When I look good you look good. When you look good, I look good. You and I are not in competition with one another. Therefore a man leave his father and his mother and cleaves to his wife and they become one flesh. That's in Genesis 2:24. Baby if I ever made you feel inferior then just know it was never my intentions."

He turned to me and for the first time in a long time, he apologized to me.

"I'm sorry baby. I've just been under a lot of stress at work. This new job is really demanding and I'm trying to do all I can to make you and the children proud."

That night we talked about a lot of things that we both had been holding in. As much as we talked, I still felt like

Eric was holding back on me. It felt good to be able to talk without yelling and getting frustrated. I fell asleep in his arms and woke up to a morning kiss. God had once again answered my prayers.

I was sitting at my desk drinking coffee when Tiffany came storming in my office.

"Guess who's going to be at the plaza tonight?" I looked up and asked,

"Who?"

"Kenny G!" Tiff said all excited.

"I wish I had known earlier. I'm going home and cook my man his favorite meal. Sheba, our nanny, is going to take the children out to eat and to a movie so we can have some alone time."

"Look at you being all romantic and what-not."

"Eric and I need this time together. He works hard. I work hard. We both need to slow down and make time for one another. So get on out of here. I plan to leave early today."

"Yes ma'am boss."

Tiffany got up and walked out the office. She was three years older than me but you would not know it. Every time I went up a level, I did all I could to make sure she elevated as well. She went from just being a Social Media Advertiser, to manager, and now she is my personal assistant on the 7th floor. I made it happen for her and I was so proud of her dedication. Tiffany stayed with me every step of the way. She had done well for a person that had no college degree. I kept trying to encourage her to go back to college and finish. I saw her potential and I wanted her to have the very best in life.

Later that evening, I was just finishing the meal I prepared for Eric and I. I had prepared baked salmon with a cranberry soy glaze, roasted asparagus, baby red potatoes, topped with a garlic butter sauce, and a tossed salad. Eric wasn't a bread eater. I loved bread. Since the children came, I had put on a few pounds more than I wanted. I had to cut back on some things and bread was one of them. I had already texted Eric to tell him to come straight home because I had prepared our dinner. What I didn't tell him was that the dinner was just for the two of us.

It was six o'clock and I had everything in place. I just knew within a few minutes Eric would be walking through the door. The table was set with China that we received as a wedding gift. I placed a beautiful centerpiece on the table with live flowers I picked up after work. The food was being kept warm and I even purchased his favorite bottle of wine. Even though I didn't drink, I made up in my mind that I was going to share a glass with him. That night we would toast to a new beginning. I just really wanted to get our marriage back on track. I was tired of the periods of silence. I was tired of the episodes of arguing. We were husband and wife. We needed to get back on the same page. I wanted us to start back having our date night and spending time with the kids together. When my father died, Eric became my shoulder to lean on. He was right there for me. He was so gentle and consoling. I don't know what I would have done if he had not been there for me. I loved Eric with my heart, mind and soul. I was his cheerleader, his prayer warrior, the mother of his children. We laughed together, cried together, prayed together. We were one! I wasn't about to let a small misunderstanding ruin the ten years we had built together.

As I was sitting at the dining room table, observing and making sure everything was in place. I spoke out loud,

"Devil you're going to have to come up with something better! You can't have my family. Back to the pits of hell you go!"

I glanced at the clock on the wall and the time was eight o'clock. I was asking myself where could he be? I had called his cell phone several times. Each time I called it went straight to voicemail. I texted him and no reply back. I called his job and they informed me he had left around five. I started to get nervous. All kinds of wild thoughts were going through my head. I started praying to God to let him be okay. I picked up my phone and started calling some of his friends. No one had heard from him or so they said. I began to pace the floor back and forth. I just knew something had happened. Time kept ticking away. Finally, I saw a light and heard a car pulling up in the drive way. I ran to the front door and opened it. It was Sheba bringing the children back home. She walked the children to the front door with a big smile on her face.

"The children really enjoyed themselves."

I was standing there looking past her and the children. Still hoping that Eric would drive up soon. I must have had a distraught look on my face. I heard Sheba asking,

"Is everything okay Mrs. Jackson?"

I was waiting for the children to come in the house. I looked at Sheba and forced a smile before I answered,

"Yes everything is great. Thank you again for doing this for me. "

"You are welcomed."

She walked back to the car and I stood there until she drove off. It was almost ten o'clock. I told the children to go get ready for bed and I would be up to check on them later. It was a Friday night. They could sleep late Saturday morning. I was on edge.

"Lord please let my husband be safe." I kept repeating it over and over.

Eleven thirty came and I heard another car pull in the driveway. I got up to walk to the front door again mumbling,

"Lord please let this be Eric. I peeped out of the window before I opened the door and sure enough it was Eric. I rushed to the door and swung it open. Eric was walking toward the entrance. I didn't give him time to come in. I ran out and met him. I fell in his arms screaming,

"Thank you Lord! Thank you God! Thank you Jesus! Baby why wouldn't you call me? I thought something had happened to you. I called your phone. I called your job."

I was going on and on. Once we made it in the house, he shut the door and asked me,

"Are the kids asleep?" I told him yes, he then told me that we needed to talk. I could tell by the expression on his face it was something serious. We both sat down on the living room sofa. I looked directly in his eyes with a questioning stare. He couldn't look me in my eyes at all. He scooted to the edge of the sofa and looked toward me. The words that came out of his mouth next change my whole life.

"I'm not happy Jae. I want a divorce. We can pick a time together to tell the kids. I'll be back sometime tomorrow to get my things. We can tell them then if you want to. I can't do this anymore. It's not that I don't love you. I'm not in love with you anymore."

I felt like a sledgehammer had came and just smashed my heart. I knew we had problems but nothing serious enough to lead to divorce. I might have felt better if I could have cried. I couldn't shed one tear. At that moment all I felt was anger and contempt. I could have killed him right then and there. I would have regretted it later, but at that moment I wanted him to die! The same woman, that just hours earlier, was praying for him to be okay, now I sat facing him wishing death on his life. I didn't beg. I didn't cry. I didn't even ask him why? I got up from the sofa, grab my cell phone, and went to my bedroom. Once I got ready to slide into my bed, I knew the old Jordyn was gone. Kudos to Satan. When he came this time, he came hard.

Chapter 6

Beast Mode

It was important for me to share my history. I needed to let you see the woman I was. I needed you to understand about my family's background. When Satan begins to launch an attack, it doesn't matter how holy or how morally grounded you think you are, if he can get you to a place where you will start listening to his lies, he will tempt you. My mistake in this whole ordeal is that I listened and followed his counsel.

The first thing I did after that dreaded night that he told me that he wanted a divorce, was call one of the missionaries from the church and told her I had some nice things I wanted to donate. I started getting trash bags and filling them up. I called Tiffany to come over and help me. His nice Armani suits, Prada shirts, his Alessandro Galet shoes priced at over two thousand dollars that I bought for his birthday. He wanted a divorce from me! I was ready to divorce him from everything. All of his brand named high price stuff was going straight to Goodwill. I was so livid with anger and hurt. I didn't wait for him to tell the children we were getting the divorce. I took it upon myself to break the news to them. It broke my heart even more when they all burst into tears. They wanted to know why daddy didn't love them anymore. I should have told them that their dad still loved them and that this had nothing to do with them. I didn't! I told them that their dad was selfish and he only thought about himself. I was so blinded by my rage until I didn't stop to think about what it was doing to the children. I wanted the children to have the same hate I felt for him.

I put in more work trying to be a good wife and a mother than I ever did at the Marketing Firm. On my job, I had to fight racism, the male constituents that were on my job that were intimidated by me and my ability to get the job done. Oh and let's not talk about the jealousy from the females that just didn't like the favor I was receiving from the big bosses. I had to come up with brilliant ideas in order to keep multi million-dollar contracts in place. Trying to be a good wife, I didn't bring my problems home. I knew Eric's job was just as demanding. I didn't want to put any more on his plate. Nobody knew what type of day I had. I left my feelings outside the door and concentrated on my family. Eric was the opposite. I could always tell when he had a bad day. He would come in all moody and snappy. I conditioned myself to just stay out of his way and prayed his mood would change. When he really got moody, as tired as I would be, I would take the kids out so he could have the house to himself. I made sacrifice after sacrifice. I was always catering to Eric and his needs. I let him make decisions as head of the household. I didn't always agree with him but I kept silent and let him take the lead. He had the audacity to bring up the fact I made more money than him. As if that was what was bothering him. I soon found out that was a lie.

I couldn't believe I have been so gullible during the course of our marriage. All those late nights at work and weekend trips out of town. It was all lies! The ink wasn't even dry on our divorce papers before he put a ring on some other woman's finger.

Mama said pray about it. Faith said pray about it. Folks at church said pray about it. Well I was done with praying about it. I had been praying since I was old enough to know what prayer was. I hadn't attended church at all while I was going through my divorce. It took three months to end what had taken ten years to build.

One Sunday, after a visit from the Pastor, I got up with the children and I got ready for church. I was running late. I really didn't have a desire to go. I wasn't ready to face the congregation with their curious stares and whispering among themselves. The church wasn't very big. If I had to guess, maybe four hundred members at any given Sunday. We walked in and just as I imagined I saw the heads looking back and even saw some whispering going on. We took our seats and I pulled out my Bible. We made it just in time. The pastor was just telling us where to turn to in our Bibles. We all stood up and were told to turn to 2 Corinthians 12:1-9. His subject was Unlimited Grace he started off by telling us that there were things that would happen in our lives that God would not remove or change. It would either humble us or change us depending on the situation. I tried my best to concentrate on the message. The more I looked around, all I could see was the decorations on my wedding day. I could see the silver bows that were placed on the front arm of each pew. My mind went back to my daddy walking me down the aisle. I remembered the music that was playing so softly. I could vision all my family and friends that came from near and far to help me celebrate. I looked across the room and I saw Eric's aunt was smiling and waving at me. She probably had been trying to get my attention. I didn't have anything personally against her. But she did raise that scoundrel of an ex-husband. She was another one telling me to pray and put it in God's hand. I felt like God had abandoned me. I was the one that played by the rules. I had come in contact with all kinds of scandalous people. They all seemed to be thriving and doing well. I don't know how long I was spaced-out in my own world. I heard the pastor inviting the congregation to The Altar for prayer. I looked at the altar. The place where Eric and I took our vows before God. It was too much for me. I motioned for my kids to get up so we could leave. Right before I exited the door, I heard the pastor say, this too shall pass, I didn't look back or break my stride.

Once I loaded the children in the car, I asked them where they wanted to eat. They all wanted to eat at a little pizza place not far from where we lived. We were sitting in the restaurant and I had just placed our order, when walking to our table were two of our neighbors. Hal and Carolyn Green were an older couple in their sixties. Carolyn started talking first.

"I'm so sorry to hear about you and Eric. I always thought the two of you were such a nice couple."

Then her husband chimed in,

"If you need anything just let us know. Eric and I would talk from time to time. He's a good man. I hate the two of you couldn't work it out."

I smiled and thanked them both for their concern. As they were walking off, I started mumbling to myself,

"Get on with that bull."

Eric was furious with me for getting rid of his clothes and other items. I didn't care. We started arguing so bad the police had to be called. The both of us were outside screaming to the top of our lungs. When the police arrived, it was Hal and Carolyn the first two on the scene. My gut feeling was that they had called the police. They allowed Eric to go in the house while I stayed outside, so he could get the rest of all of his things. He didn't even have that much left. One of the officers told Eric that he would have to make a police report and take me to court to get any other items. My parents taught me a lot. One thing they taught me was never throw away your receipts. Over half of the stuff, he was complaining about was bought by me. He knew it. That police report never was made and I didn't go to court at least not for that.

Eric had blocked me from all his social media accounts. I wasn't able to see any of his activities. So, I made a Facebook dummy account with a fake name. His page wasn't open to the public but his new fiancé's page was. Tiffany helped me to find out her name. I would sit in my bed and just scroll through her page. I saw pictures of her and him together. Every time I saw a new picture it would further fuel the rage in me. I would sit up and imagine him having a bad car wreck and dying. I would imagine her and him burning up in a house fire. I know it sounds evil and it was evil thinking. I'm just trying to get you to see just how dark and sinister hate and anger will take you. I stopped communicating with my mother and sister as much. I didn't want to hear anything from anybody about how God will see me through all of this. I was done with trying to do things the right way. The right way got me done the wrong way.

The judge gave Eric visitation rights every other weekend. I didn't want him anywhere near my babies. If he loved them so much he never would have walked away and left them. The first couple of times he came to pick them up we cut up with each other so bad we ended back up in court. Eric's aunt had started picking them up and taking them to her house. From there, Eric picked the children up and dropped them back off there. Every time they came back home I would pick them for information. Then I would turn around and get mad once they tell me.

They seemed to like their dad's new bride-to-be. I didn't want them to like him and I sure didn't want them to like her. Eric Jr started acting out in school. His grades were failing and he was constantly getting into fights. I took absolutely no accountability for what was happening with my children. Anything that went wrong, I blamed it all on Eric. He was the villain. A modern-day Darth Vader. If I could have killed him myself and got away with it I think I would have.

Chapter 7

Self-Destruction

I was sitting at the bar with Tiffany on a Friday night. It was Eric's weekend with the kids and I took advantage of it. Remember the woman that didn't drink? She was now drinking on the regular. I broke out of the shell and became a totally new woman. Tiffany said she knew I had it in me all the time. I just had to break loose. I was going to be thirty-six on my next birthday. There I was, thirty-five years old before I took my first alcoholic drink. It took some getting used too. I couldn't just chuckle it down like Tiffany. She was a pro at drinking. I would get on the dance floor and dance until my feet hurt. I met a lot of cute guys. I didn't hesitate to let them know that I was single and I wanted to mingle. I would talk about Eric to whoever would listen. I called him all kind of names. He was sorry, pathetic, a cheat and a liar. I would get so drunk that my speech became slurred. I could barely stand up straight.

I don't know how Tiffany did it but she managed to get us home safely every time we hit that bar. At first, I only went on the weekends that Eric had the kids. Then I started going every weekend and would pay for a babysitter for the kids. I had gotten to where I couldn't sleep at night unless I had been drinking. My doctor prescribed me some sleeping pills to help me out. I developed a taste for wine. Through the week after work I always poured me a glass. It would relax me and take away tension from my body.

I was sitting on the bar stool in the kitchen while sipping on Chardonnay. I popped open my laptop to see what Brittany had posted lately. Britney was my ex's new found love. There was a picture with him and her engaged in a kiss. The caption was,

"We're having a baby."

I almost dropped my glass of wine. We hadn't even been divorced a good six months and they were already starting a family. I took another sip of my wine and yelled at the computer.

"I hope it dies or comes out retarded!" It was a very ugly thing to say. But to be honest, I didn't care. I couldn't understand how the man that inflicted so much pain on me got to be so happy. I called Tiffany up on a week night,

"Hello."

"Hi do you want to hit the bar tonight?"

"I'm game what time?"

"Let me see if I can get Sheba to come and watch the kids. I'll hit you back up."

"Sure thing."

I called and she was able to come and watch the children. I went upstairs to my bedroom to shower and change. I stood watching my reflection in the bathroom mirror. I began to wonder what was so special about Britney that would make Eric want to leave me. I had put on a couple of pounds after giving birth to my children. I had even developed stretch marks. Had I become unattractive to him? I started running my fingers through my shoulder length hair. I had wanted to cut it for some time. Eric always told me not to. He loved to play with my hair. All of a sudden I started feeling ugly. I didn't wear a lot of makeup. I wore only the bare minimum. I walked over to my closet and took a look at my clothes. I realize the majority of my clothing was work attire. I didn't have anything that was sexy or appealing. I needed some clothes that would bring me out. Tiffany wore revealing clothes every time we went out. As long as we had been friends, I never asked her why she never remarried. She told me she married once and she too had gotten her heart broken.

These men aren't worth the aggravation. I said to myself another night at the bar. Tiffany and I turned the shot glasses up. The bar had become my getaway. The alcohol was my numbing mechanism to soothe the pain I was enduring. That night I had gotten too intoxicated. I couldn't even get up to make it to work. I got up to get the children off to school and I saw they were already gone. My head was banging. I felt sick to my stomach. Sheba was washing up dishes in the sink. She turned around to greet me as I staggered to the kitchen table and plopped down in the chair.

"I made you some coffee Mrs. Jackson."

I had my eyes closed rubbing the front of my head. I opened my eyes to see her standing in front of me handing me the cup.

"When did you come in?" I asked.

"I never left you were kind of out of it last night. I stayed to make sure the children would get to school on time."

"Thank you Sheba. This won't ever happen again at least not during the weekdays."

"I'm going to go home now. I'll pick the children up as usual. Would you like me to prepare the meal today or are you going to cook?"

"Yes, I mean no. You come in and do the things like you regularly do them"

" Yes ma'am. I'll see you later today."

After she left, I crawled back into bed and fell asleep. I was awakened by the constant ringing of my cell phone. I grabbed it from the nightstand and saw it was Tiffany.

"Hello did you forget the meeting you had scheduled for today?"

"Dang Tiff! I forgot all about it. What time is it now?"

"It's 12:30."

"Tiff how are you able to get up and go to work after drinking all night?"

"I'm just used to it."

"Look see if you can reschedule that meeting. Tell them I came down with a stomach bug or something."

"Will do!"

"And Tiff, I owe you girl."

"No problem boss."

God always give us warning before destruction. He had given me plenty but I was too caught up in my despair to pay attention. Everything worked out. Tiffany was able to reschedule the meeting. All things were back on track. We did our usual weekend bar escape.

Sunday afternoon I was resting on the couch when the doorbell rang. The kids were with Eric and it wasn't time for them to be home yet. I got up to go to the door. I peeped out of the curtains and there were five ladies from the church standing there. I was not ready to deal with any of them. I had not been back to church since the day I walked out. That was over three months ago. Before I opened the door, I had to take a deep breath. I was not in the mood for those ladies. I opened the door and tried my best to muster up a smile.

"Sis Jackson how are you doing?" The first lady asked.

"I'm good." I replied.

"Do you mind if we come in and visit with you?" It was the same lady speaking. I opened the door wider and invited them in. I saw they had something with aluminum foil wrapped around it.

"Sis Lettie baked you a caramel cake. She told us to make sure we gave it to you."

I took the cake from the one lady that was holding it and I told them to have a seat. I walked in the kitchen to put the cake on the counter. I heard one of the ladies say, she has a beautiful home. Then another lady was saying it looks like one of those houses you see in Better Homes & Garden Magazine. I walked back in the room and asked them in a nice voice,

"What can I do for you ladies today?"

I knew every last one of them. They were members of the missionary Society at my church. Sister Gladys the first one that greeted me at the door, started talking.

"Well sister Jackson we know you haven't been coming to church lately. Pastor said he had been calling and left you several messages, he said you hadn't returned any of his calls. Even came by a couple of times but he said there was no answer. So he asked us to come by and check on you. We just wanted you to know that we are your family. If you need us, just let us know. Today we would be happy to pray for you or with you. We can even do Bible study if you like. "

I was taught to always respect my elders. I decided not to tell these group of ladies what I really wanted to say, which was get out. So instead I made up a lie so nobody's feelings would be hurt.

"I'm glad you stopped by today but I'm really not feeling well. I have a bad headache. All I want to do is get some rest and maybe I can shake this headache. Keep praying for me but right now I just want to be alone."

They just gave each other this look of being appalled by what I said. I still didn't care. I wanted them out of my house. As they got up to leave, I told them to thank Sister Lettie for the cake and make sure they call before they came again.

All my life, I heard you got to "watch how you do God's people." I was God's people. Look how my ex-husband did me. He was still up enjoying life and doing his thing. Hell and brimstone hadn't consumed him yet. I was beginning to wonder was there even such thing as God.

Later on that night as I was getting ready for bed, my phone rang. I picked it up and saw that it was Faith. I went on an answered since I had ignored her other six phone calls.

"What's up Faith?"

"What's up with you? And why haven't you been answering me and mama's phone calls?"

"I've been busy."

"Too busy to answer the phone or reply back to a text? Mom has been worried out of her mind. We are coming to see you and the kids next weekend."

As soon as she made that statement I quickly came up with something to detour her.

"Faith I'm working on a big project at work that has me working every weekend even on Sundays. That's why I haven't been returning any calls. By the time I make it home all I can do is eat and hit the bed?"

Lying had become my second language. The lies just rolled off my tongue.

"Jae we are family. I know the divorce was hard on you. But you can't keep distancing yourself from the people that genuinely love and care for you. Don't give Eric that kind of power."

Faith had struck a nerve, " I'm not giving Eric anything!" I shouted. " I told you I was busy with my job. What does Eric have to do with my job Faith?"

"Listen at you. I can hear it all in your voice."

"You don't hear anything in my voice!"

"Jae I'm going to keep praying for you. You need help. When you're ready call us we will be here for you."

I didn't even say bye. I just hung up the phone. The nerve of her! Talking about don't give Eric that type of power. Eric didn't have any power over me. I started trying to rationalize the conversation in my head. They didn't know about anything I was feeling. She still had Tyrone. She was forced to get married because she got pregnant. I got the husband first and look what has happened to me. Faith was the last person to try to tell me anything about a divorce.

I hope you are seeing how the enemy blinds you to the truth. I was blinded or maybe I wasn't ready to accept the truth.

The weekend rolled around again. Tiffany wasn't feeling like going out that Friday. I decided to go out on my own. It was Eric's weekend with the kids and I decided to do it up right. I missed Tiffany being with me but I knew some of the regulars that hung out. I limited my drinking because I was going to have to drive myself. At least that's what I told myself. There were so many guys offering to buy me drinks, I told myself I didn't want to disappoint them. I laughed and flirted the whole time I was there. It was like all my problems and pains just magically disappeared. I felt free. It was the part of my life I had been missing out on. I enjoyed the calming euphoria.

I was fumbling for my keys in my purse. I found them and I was stumbling to get to my car. My head was reeling from the alcohol. For a few minutes, I rested my head on the headrest in my car. I just needed a few minutes. Tiffany always got us home safely and she drank more than me. I crank the car up and let the window down to get some air, this is something that I had seen Tiffany do often. I made it out in the traffic and I thought I was doing pretty good. After maybe 10 minutes into driving, blue lights were behind me. I was wondering what I had done. I pulled over, look out of the rear view mirror and saw the officer coming to my driver's side. I quickly looked for a peppermint but I couldn't find one. The officer knocked on my window and I let it down.

"What seems to be the problem officer?" I asked him in the most calm voice that I could muster up. His replied,

"Mam you ran a red light back there. Can I see your license and registration please" I fumbled around in my purse until I found my license. I reached over to my glove compartment to get my registration papers. He left with my license and told me he would be right back. He came back and handed me my license and registration. He was writing me out of ticket. I may have gotten away with just a ticket if I hadn't ran my big mouth.

"Sir are you really going to give me a ticket? Who did I hurt? Nobody!"

As soon as I started running my mouth he asked me had I been drinking. I started shaking my head wildly. The next thing I knew, I was told to step out of the car. He brought the breathalyzer around. I was told to blow in it and I did. Before long, I was handcuffed, sitting in the back of a police car headed to jail. In my head, I was pleading for God to help me. I know what you're thinking, now she wants to call on God. Yes I did. I needed his help.

Chapter 8

Revelation

It was Saturday morning when I woke up in a jail cell. I looked around and there were other females in the cell with me. I felt terrible but it wasn't from the alcohol. It was from the predicament I had gotten myself into. I thought about my children and Sheba. They must have been worried out of their minds. There was one younger girl that looked friendly. I asked her were we allowed to make phone calls. She said we could but it wouldn't do any good because the judge won't be back until Monday. I started to panic. There was no way I could stay locked up until Monday. I started searching my brains as to who I could call. Tiffany was the only person I could think of. I had been so mean and ugly to people. I doubted if any of them would come to my rescue. I kept talking to myself. Think Jordyn think! Who can you call to get you out before Monday morning? Nobody on my job because this would be a stain on my work record.

I started talking to God in my head. I was pleading and begging him to tell me what to do. Who could I call? There was only one person I knew that could possibly get me out of that jail before Monday. I had to think about it. I was in a desperate situation. The words from the pastor's last sermon hit my spirit.

God allows things to happen either to humble us or change us. At that moment, I had no choice but to humble myself. I called for the jailer. He came to the cell and I asked him if I could have my phone call. He stood there with a smirk on his face before he said,

"Lady it won't do you any good. You're stuck here for the weekend. There won't be a judge here until Monday morning."

I was trying hard not to get agitated. I spoke slowly and softly.

"Sir if you would just let me make my phone call please."

He took the keys unlock the door and told me to follow him. There was another officer sitting behind a desk.

"What is she about to do?" He asked in an arrogant tone. The jailer replied,

"Waste a phone call."

I dialed the number and prayed that Eric would pick up he did and accepted the phone call.

"Eric it's me Jordyn. I need you to come and get me out of jail."

"Jail! What did you do?"

"I got a DUI."

"D.U.I? Jae you don't even drink!"

"Eric listen to me, if you don't come and get me, I have to stay here until Monday morning."

What precinct are you at?"

The one on 11th and 10th station 9, I think." I started to cry.

"Hold on Jae, I'm on the way."

The call cut off. I hung up the phone feeling somewhat relieved. If Eric had not accepted the call, I deserved it. I had been so caught up in destroying him until I didn't realize I was destroying myself. I was back in the jail cell. I started asking God to forgive me for all the ugly evil things I had said and done. I talked about Eric being evil but he was the one that had the heart to come and get me. The only one I could call. Maybe God had set it up that way. It wasn't even an hour when I heard the jailer say,

"Jordyn Jackson you made bail."

I jumped up and I couldn't wait to walk out of that jail cell.

"I guess I was wrong. It must be nice to have pull in high places. "

I didn't even take the time to respond. Eric was standing in the front of the jail waiting on me. I retrieved all of my items, Eric and I just walked out the door to his car. I got in and breathed a sigh of relief. I heard Eric ask was I okay. I just nodded my head and the tears begin to fall down my face. Eric reached in the glove compartment and handed me some Kleenex.

"I'm going to get you a lawyer. You may have to pay a fine. It's your first offense so you won't have to do any jail time."

I was so choked up the only thing I could say was, "Thank you." Eric didn't bombard me with any questions I appreciated it. I wasn't ready to answer any questions. When we pulled up in my driveway, I thanked him once again before I got out. He simply said,

"You're welcome."

The minute I got in the house, I went upstairs and got in the shower. I cried the whole time I was in there. As soon as I got out and got dressed, I found my Bible and turned to Psalms 51 and I began to read. I couldn't stop the tears from flowing from my eyes. I had left the protecting and comforting arms of my loving God to the arms of a devil that almost destroyed me. I allowed him to take control of my thoughts. I dance by his music for peace. I never had peace in my heart all the while I listened to him. Stepping out of the will of God is the worst thing a person can do. I prayed once again. I was still asking God for his forgiveness.

I called Tiffany to tell her what happened. I stressed to her the importance of nobody finding out on the job. I made her promise not to say anything to anybody. Our conduct on the outside could have an effect on how our clients view us. Going out for drinks wasn't against company policy. But doing anything that could go on your record was another story. A D.U.I. could cause the clients to wonder if you were capable of properly handling their account. I was hoping and praying that my job never found out about it.

Monday morning and my team and I were at it. We were all sitting around the table brainstorming. Mr. Kapp came to the door and told me he needed to talk to me. I left my notes with Tiffany and told her to take over until I got back. I stepped outside the door and Mr. Kapp told me I needed to go to the 9th floor. Mr Brooks wanted to talk to me. I was curious to know what he wanted with me. It was very seldom that any of us got to talk to him one-on-one. We had a chain of command. I reported to Mr. Kapp and Mr. Kapp had somebody he reported to before you got to Mr. Brooks or Mr. Bracs.

I made it to the 9th floor. I went to the door that had his name on it. I knocked and his receptionist asked me my name. I told her Jordyn Jackson. Then she told me to go right on in. I walked in this very huge and impeccably decorated office. He looked up briefly and told me to take a seat. I sat down waiting for him to say something. He didn't start talking right away. Finally, he looked up from the papers he had in his hand.

"Mrs. Jackson,"

I cleared my throat to answer,

"Sir?"

"It has been brought to my attention that you had a little brush with the law over the weekend. Is this true?"

I was so shocked and gotten away with, at first, I honestly didn't know what to say. I was honest with God when I asked him to restore me and bring me back into his presence. I told Mr. Brooks the truth.

"Yes sir it is. I went out to have some drinks and I had a few too many. I tried to drive home, ran a red light, got pulled over and went to jail for driving intoxicated."

I started wondering how did he find out so fast. Had Eric called my job told them just to hurt me? Tiffany would definitely never say anything so I know it had to be Eric. What was the point of him even bailing me out if he was going to turn around and try to get me fired from my job.

"I thank you for your honesty. We here at Brooks and Bracs pride ourselves on honesty and loyalty as every company should. I haven't heard anything but good things about you since you've been here. I may not always mingle all the time with the employees, trust me when I tell you. I know more than you think about what goes on."

I was thinking all the while he was talking. 'Just go ahead and fire me, I messed up and I have no one to blame but myself.'

"Jordyn, may I call you Jordyn?"

"Yes sir."

"I was informed how you went to bat for a young lady named Tiffany Royce."

I blurted out, "She's a great worker!"

"Great worker she may be but not such a loyal worker."

I wasn't understanding where he was coming from.

"Sir with all due respect, I can't think of anything that she has done or would do to hurt this company."

"Can you think of anything she would do to hurt you?"

I started shaking my head.

"No sir, Tiffany and I have been working together for ten years. My children call her Tee-tee Tiffany!"

Mr. Brock leaned back in his chair and gave me a look of pity.

"Jordyn it was Tiffany Royce that informed Mr Kapp of your unfortunate incident over the weekend."

I almost fell out of my chair. I was speechless. I couldn't believe that Tiffany would back-stab me the way she did.

"Makes you angry doesn't it Jordyn? The only reason I'm telling you this is because I know what you did for her. If she would try and sabotage your position here, after all you did for her. I can only imagine what she would do for our company. I can't fire her for saying something about another employee that was true. You chose her as your personal assistant. And you can change your personal assistant whenevr you get ready. And since Tiffany doesn't have a college degree we can place her anywhere in the company we deem fit for her. Just a little something I thought you should know."

"So I'm not fired?"

"Fired? Jordyn we need you to keep bringing clients in. You're too talented for me to fire!"

"Thank you sir."

I got up to leave and he said,

"By the way, I got that little situation taken care of. I made some phone calls and you don't have to worry about that DUI charge. It's as if it never happened."

I started crying,

"Thank you Mr. Brooks!"

"No thank you Jordyn for being a valuable member of our team."

When I made it down to the elevator, I had to stop and thank God. His grace had kept me covered. Everyone in the boardroom had left. I walked into my office and their Tiffany was sitting at her desk. She looked up and saw I had been crying.

"Oh my God. What happened?"

I looked back at her as I was walking by and told her I didn't want to talk about it. I tried to remain cordial to her throughout the rest of the day. An hour before time for us to leave, I went to her desk and told her that she needed to get all of her stuff out because I was getting another assistant. She became so dramatic.

"Why? What did I do? I didn't say anything to anybody about anything?"

She was telling off on herself. It seemed like the people I trusted the most we're always letting me down. And the people that actually cared about me, I pushed them away. One thing I knew I had to do. I had to apologize to a lot of people.

Chapter 9

Redemption

I realize now that my divorce was my thorn in my flesh. No matter how much I prayed to God. I couldn't stop the progress. Many things had happened in my life that I could eventually fix. But Eric leaving me was something that was out of my control. Instead of just letting go and letting God handle it, I became bitter and spiteful. I wanted him to hurt just like I was hurting. I didn't want to forgive. I wanted to hang on to that anger. I was wounded but I refused to stay with the source that could heal me. I wanted to be the one that was in control of my situation. It was out of my hands and I felt powerless. I became driven by a spirit of defiance that had me in attack mode. Eye for an eye, tooth for a tooth so to speak.

God put me in a position that woke me up to the truth, sitting in a jail cell doesn't work for everybody but it worked for me. Our heavenly Father knows what it takes to get his children back in alignment with Him. To be back in the arms of God was the best feeling I had ever had. He didn't leave me. I left Him. His amazing grace kept me covered even in my darkest moment of life.

I had people I had to go to in order to make amends. My family, my church family, and yes even Eric. I painted him as the monster. The evil one out of all of this. Yet he was the one I had to call on when I couldn't call anyone else. I still don't agree with how he up and left the children and I. I have now come to realize that I had to let God deal with Eric. Vengeance is mine saith the Lord. I wanted to be the Avenger.

I re-dedicated my life back to God one Sunday morning during worship service. The same church I walked out of, with the same people I had been so ugly too. They welcomed me back with open arms. This time I welcomed their prayers. I cried like a baby standing at the altar. I felt hands on my shoulders, my back and on my head. The prayers were powerful. The more the tears ran down my face, the more I could feel the tension and anxiety easing from my body.

Just looking at me you wouldn't have been able to tell anything was wrong with me. My wounds were internal. Only those that really knew me could tell something was wrong by my actions. It's true that hurt people hurt other people. I was still in love with Eric. I can admit that now. My pain was stemming from the fact that he didn't love me anymore. Maybe I should say that he didn't love me enough to stay with me. I was jealous because he found someone else to love. I started doubting myself, I hung out at the bars so I could just drink and get the attention of other men. They complimented me and made me feel desirable again. Those men weren't looking for a relationship they were looking for a good time.

I wish I could end my story by telling you that I had found me a good man. The truth is that I'm taking time to let God work on me. I'm still working on letting my anger subside. All the negative emotions I had been feeling haven't went away. I would love to have another companion. But right now I'm just not in the right place to give another man what he deserves. Jumping into another relationship carrying old hurts from the past is a recipe for disaster. That's my opinion. I'm going to concentrate on me for a while. God blessed me with three beautiful babies that are depending on me. Those three little faces are the best thing that came out of my marriage. I'm glad that my parents taught me how to survive. I strayed but thanks to God I didn't stay. I came back to my teaching. I came back to my faith. I came back to my peace, love and joy. I came back to God. I'll never leave the safety of His arms again.

I'm Jordan Layla Jackson and I pray that you were inspired by my story.

AUTHOR MELISSA HAMLETT

From the Author's Desk
For 15 years now I have been teaching and preaching the gospel
of Jesus Christ. I thank God for His divine wisdom and love that
has carried me through every twist and turn I found myself facing
in life
I want to thank God for my three loving children Chantineia,
Justin, and Taja. These are my three heartbeats that made every
challenge worth it.
I also thank and appreciate the rest of my family and friends
that supported and encouraged me to step out on faith.
Zechariah 4:10....Do not despise small beginnings. I appreciate
everything God has done,
is doing, and is about to do. Not only in my life but in your
lives as well.
Blessings to all.